W9-BWS-067

3 1160 00376 5554

$\mathcal{L}$OOKING *for* ANGELS

by VALISKA GREGORY *illustrated by* LESLIE BAKER

SIMON & SCHUSTER BOOKS FOR YOUNG READERS

"For my bonny daughters, Melissa and Holly"

—V. G.

"For Stephanie Owens Lurie"

—L. B.

SIMON & SCHUSTER BOOKS FOR YOUNG READERS
An imprint of Simon & Schuster Children's Publishing Division
1230 Avenue of the Americas
New York, New York 10020
Text copyright © 1996 by Valiska Gregory
Illustrations copyright © 1996 by Leslie Baker
All rights reserved including the right of reproduction
in whole or in part in any form.
SIMON & SCHUSTER BOOKS FOR YOUNG READERS
is a trademark of Simon & Schuster.
Book design by Lucille Chomowicz.
The text for this book is set in 18-point Cochin.
The illustrations are rendered in watercolor.
Manufactured in the United States of America
First Edition
10 9 8 7 6 5 4 3 2 1

Library of Congress Cataloging-in-Publication Data
Gregory, Valiska.
Looking for angels / by Valiska Gregory ; illustrated by Leslie Baker.
p.   cm. Summary: Sarah's grandfather shows her how to look for the sleeping sun,
jewels in the garden, a circus outside the window, and angels.
[1. Grandfathers—Fiction. 2. Imagination—Fiction.] I. Baker, Leslie A.,
ill. II. Title. PZ7.G8624Lo 1996 [E]—dc20 94-34341 CIP AC
ISBN 0-689-80500-4

"Try to be one of the people on whom nothing is lost!"
—HENRY JAMES

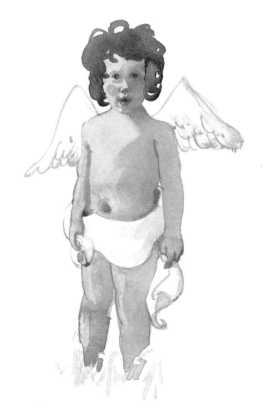

"Remember," said Sarah's grandpa as he tucked in the quilt, "tomorrow we'll be looking for angels."

Sarah laughed and wrinkled her nose. "It sounds pretty silly to me."

"You never know just when an angel might appear," Grandpa said, "so you'll have to be careful not to miss a thing."

No matter what her grandpa said, the next morning Sarah expected a perfectly ordinary day, plain as a brown sparrow. But that is definitely not what Sarah got.

When Sarah came into the kitchen for breakfast, Grandpa was waiting.

"I hope you didn't miss the morning sun," he said. "It sometimes sleeps on the four-poster bed."

"But the sun can't sleep," said Sarah.

"It sometimes seems to," he said. "If I were you, I'd look again."

So Sarah did.

Like the yellow-eyed cat, all whiskery and warm,
the sunlight on the rumpled quilt
purred its patchwork dreams and yawned.

"You were right," Sarah said. "The sun was curled up on the bed with the cat."

"Maybe you didn't see it at first because you weren't awake enough."

"Maybe."

Sarah plopped a fresh raspberry in her mouth and grinned. "I haven't seen an angel yet."

"I expect not," said Grandpa, "but then, I think you did miss the jewels in my garden."

Sarah turned around and looked again.

Red rubies glittered on thorny stems
and butterflies winked through a crown
of emerald leaves and marigolds.

"Sometimes," Grandpa said, "the dewdrops on the spider's web look like diamonds."

"Not real diamonds."

"Still, they're quite a treasure."

Sarah sprinkled ruby-raspberries over her cereal while Grandpa poured the milk. "But we didn't see an angel," she said.

"No, we didn't," said Grandpa. "On the other hand, I hope you saw the circus outside the window."

"What circus?" asked Sarah. She took a closer look.

A squirrel tiptoed across a high-wire branch
while down below, just like a silly clown,
a nuthatch skittered up and down the trunk.

Sarah and her grandpa sat together in the dappled sun.

"Of course," said Sarah, "it wasn't really a circus."

"No, but it was just as interesting."

"And we still haven't seen an angel," she said.

"No, we haven't. But did you notice that rabbit eating noodles?"

"Rabbits don't eat noodles!"

"Well, not quite," said Grandpa, "but I think you ought to have a look."

The rabbit neatly nipped a blade of grass
and as he ate, green inch by noodle inch,
it disappeared beneath his twitching nose.

Sarah fetched the newspaper as her grandpa poured the lemonade. She stopped to watch a honeybee cradled in the petals of a rose.

"You know," she said, "that rabbit was just a baby."

Grandpa smiled. "When you were a baby, you looked just like an angel."

"Not a real angel," Sarah said. "I can prove it."

Sarah went to the bookcase and got the
encyclopedia that began with the letter A.

She turned the pages past the picture of an
aardvark, past *acorn* and *acrobat,* and even past the
map of *Alaska,* until she got to the pictures of
angels.

"Now look at these," Sarah said. She showed
her grandpa angels made of stone and angels with
wings white as moths.

They looked at plump cherub angels and angels with golden trumpets. There were angels no bigger than the head of a pin and angels as tall as the clouds.

"Now these are what I call angels," Sarah said.

"Those are angels all right," said Grandpa, "but I was looking for an everyday angel—the kind most people don't take time to see."

"But you *can't* see . . ." Sarah stopped. She thought about how she'd missed the yellow-eyed sun and the jewels in the garden, missed the circus and the baby rabbit.

Then Sarah looked very hard at the far side of the garden where the honeysuckle grew.

"Grandpa, come quick," she whispered. "I think it's an angel!"

A hummingbird, bluegreen and shimmering,
wings quickening faster than the eye can see,
hovered, like grace, between the earth and sky.